HAGGIS THE DRAGON

Book 1

**Written and illustrated by
Victoria Chalker**

VICTORIA CHALKER

All proceeds that come to the author from this book go directly to the Chilterns MS Centre

Registered Charity number **800853**

Haggis help - to give more go to:

http://uk.virginmoneygiving.com/ SomeoneSpecial/Haggishelp

Edition 2
Copyright © 2015 Victoria Chalker
All rights reserved.

ISBN-10: 1500133906

ISBN-13: 978-1500133900

For Alice Maureen Jackson, who loved to paint.

DINGCATS

Someone has to

VICTORIA CHALKER

This book belongs to a little dragon called

....

....

HAGGIS THE DRAGON

 Once upon a time there was a boy aged 8, named Miles

He lived with his Mum and Dad, a black and white cat with white socks on each foot

….and his little sister Pip.

One night Miles couldn't sleep. He lay listening to Dad snoring away.

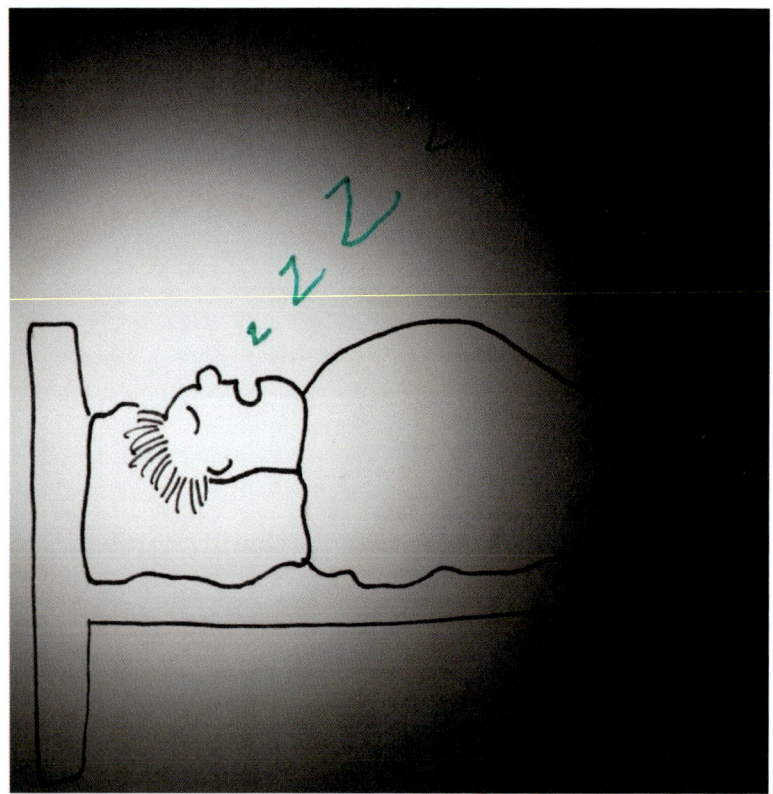

BANG.

A huge noise smashed through the night. A little scared Miles cautiously peeped out of his bedroom window.

To his amazement he saw two giant golden eyes, a long nose and clouds of smoke.

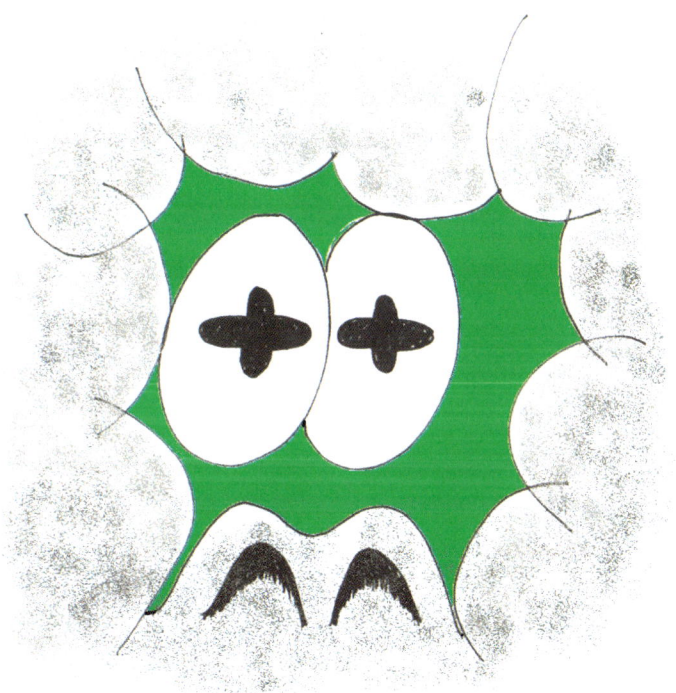

"Hello, I'm Haggis" said the dragon. "Would you like to go for a ride?"

"Er" said Miles wondering how much trouble he'd be in if Mum found out and how much fun it may be.

"Yes please, I think I would."

"Climb on!" said Haggis.

Haggis put his head on the bedroom floor and Miles clambered onto his neck. It was very comfortable. He held tight to the scales. Haggis raised his head and out they went.

"Where shall we go?" Asked Haggis.

"Everywhere?!" said Miles

Haggis bent to take off, Miles shouted "Wait!!!! Can Pip come too?"

"Yes" said Haggis. They walked round the house and knocked gently on her window.

"Am I dreaming?" she yawned as she saw the beautiful green dragon with golden scales and yellow wings.

"No." said Miles grinning from ear to ear.

"He's real. Quick climb on and don't wake Mum and Dad or we'll be for it!"

Once Pip had clambered up Haggis bent his legs, lifted his wings and ...

WHOOSH.

Up

Up

Up

they went into the night sky.

They flew over houses, the school yard, the park, the fire station, rivers and towns. They saw tiny white lights of cars on the motorway and boats on the sea.

VICTORIA CHALKER

The dark shape of a volcano got closer and closer.

"Is that where we're going?" shouted Pip through the wind. "Yes" said Haggis. "That's where I live, my volcano lair."

Suddenly they started down fast,

ZOOooooom.

THUD!

They landed on a ledge that led into a cave in the volcano.

"Haggis....is that you?" came a screeching roar "I told you to tidy your pod before you could play. There are embers everywhere!"

Just then a huge head popped out of the cave. Miles and Pip nearly fell off Haggis in surprise. It belonged to a red dragon with blue spots and incredibly elegant wings.

"Oooooh, you naughty little dragonpop - you never said we had friends for dinner."

"Sorry Mum, can they stay, please?" said Haggis

"Ok" she said, "but you can cook."

Miles and Pip scrambled down, jumping over the two swishing tails and went into the cave.

It was amazing, there were lights all around made from burning moss on sticks, pictures on the walls of dragons, flying and breathing fire, and in the centre of the room was a pile of sticks with a pan on top.

"Are you hungry?" asked Haggis. He breathed onto the sticks then a large fire roared. The pan bubbled and burbled.

"How much would you like? How much do snaffles eat?" he said. Miles and Pip had never had dinner with dragons before and did not know what was in the pot.

"What exactly is for dinner?" asked Miles.

"What exactly are snaffles?"

Pip edged closer holding Miles' hand.

"Ahahahahahahahaaaaa" laughed Haggis and his Mum. "Dragon food of course – what do you think we eat?"

"Cows" said Pip as quick as a flash, "and sheep and goats and pigs too, and people who miss the last bus home!"

"We eat no such thing," said Haggis. "In this lair dragons eat mushy fruit and vegetables and special volcanic rocks, to help us breathe fire. You are the snaffles. Uncle Boris always calls little squeekers snaffles. He says they are good for filling in gaps between meals so I thought I would see if you would play."

"Oh" said Miles, "I'll try mush then please, but no fire breathing rocks thank you, I'm not sure my dentist would like it."

Pip had nothing to eat, she sat as near to Miles as she could and watched mesmerised as the others ate. Haggis and his mum had rocks for pudding!

Afterwards Haggis said "Can you play clawball? I love to play but Mum is always too busy doing grown-up things and I could do with a new goalie."

"I've never played clawball but I have played football" said Miles "and Pip is a demon goalie."

They set themselves up on the ledge, using the cave entrance as the goal.

Pip was a bit wary at first of the 12 foot dragon charging towards her, it was very hard to get used to kicking and catching a ball up to her waist.

It was 2-1 to Miles and he needed one more goal to win. He aimed for the goal and kicked his biggest kick. The mega ball soared past Pip and bounced off the edge of the cave. It zoomed back, just missing Miles and plummeted over the ledge.

"Oh no" wailed Pip "the ball is gone, I am so sorry Haggis, I couldn't catch it."

Haggis did not speak at all, he just dropped backwards off the ledge. Miles and Pip ran and on their tummies leaned their heads over. The saw him shoot like a rocket, wings tucked in tight, then catch the ball in his teeth and sweep round back up to the ledge.

Just at that moment his Mum came out.

"Haggis, get those snaffles away from that edge. I have enough mess to clear up inside and don't want more thank you very much. I think it's time you took them home."

"Come on" he said, "I'll take you home before it gets light." and they clambered onto his strong neck.

"Bye Mum" he called leaping off the ledge.

Down

Down

Down

they swept, across the fields and along the river, back above the houses.

THUMP.

They landed at home.

Haggis gently lowered Miles and Pip, they scrambled down. Pip yawned "Thanks Haggis, will you ever come again?"

He did not hear, with a "Good night snaffles" he bent his legs, lifted his wings and took off.

They both watched until he was just a tiny speck in the sky and then crawled into bed.

HAGGIS THE DRAGON

The next day a scream woke them "What has happened to my car?" shouted Dad.

They looked out of the window. Two footprints were squashed into the roof of Dad's car.

"How did those get there?" said Mum.

Miles looked at Pip and winked "I know, perhaps it was the dragon we rode last night?"

"A dragon?" said Dad

"A dragon?" said Mum, "Don't be silly, everyone knows there are no such things as dragons."

Haggis & Miles say goodbye

All proceeds that come to the author from this book go directly to the Chilterns MS Centre

The Chilterns MS Centre provides drug-free symptom management therapies for people with Multiple Sclerosis Each week around 350 people visit the Centre for treatment such as physiotherapy, hydrotherapy and oxygen treatment and engender a sociable atmosphere and offer an opportunity for people with multiple sclerosis to get help and help themselves.

Registered charity address
Oakwood Close, Wendover
Aylesbury, Buckinghamshire, HP22 5LX
Registered Charity number **800853**

Haggis help - to give more go to:

HTTP://UK.VIRGINMONEYGIVING.COM/SOMEONESPECIAL/HAGGISHELP

HAGGIS THE DRAGON

Haggis and the mermaid

Book 2

VICTORIA CHALKER

Do you have a story in mind for Haggis?

ABOUT THE AUTHOR

Victoria Chalker works in a secret government laboratory – she could tell you what she does but then you would have to work there too.

She lives in Bedfordshire with her family, cat Toby and 6 ducks called Quackers, Lucky, Chloe, Gustard, Bigfoot and Crispy. Her two children have helped with Haggis the Dragon - the first book she has written for children. You may sometimes see her on a train or plane doodling for the latest book.

Printed in Great Britain
by Amazon